This book belongs to

_____

ISBN 978-1-9196356-0-6

Illustrations by Tatiana Mazanko

Edited By: R Nketia

Published by: Kofi and Adjoa's Stories

For all enquiries email:

Kofiandadjoastories@gmail.com

www.kofiandadjoasstories.com

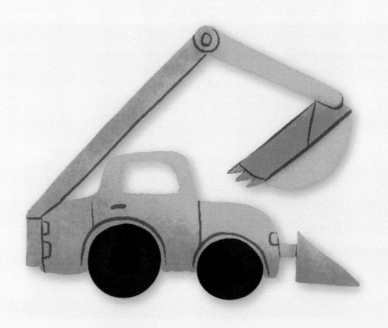

Dedicated to my one and only Mother Rose and my son Avraham-Alexavier also known as Kofi. Your funny bedtime scenarios along with the bond and love between you both inspired every part of this story.

Kofi and Adjoa like to stay at Grandma's house, they love to jump on her huge bed.

They ask Grandma to read their favorite book and listen attentively.

Grandma tells Kofi and Adjoa to say their bedtime prayer.

Adjoa falls asleep straight away but Kofi is **wide awake!**

"Lie down Kofi, I am going to tidy up. When I have finished, I will come and lie down with you," Grandma says.

Kofi frowns and says,

Okay Grandma!

Grandma begins to hoover the living room, when suddenly she notices Kofi's yellow digger on the floor.

Who put this here?

Grandma looks around and there is no one there. She puts it back into the toy box and continues to tidy up.

Grandma picks up the shoes to put them on the shoe rack, when suddenly, she notices that all of the coats have dropped.

In the kitchen, Grandma puts on her music using her tablet and starts washing the dishes. Then suddenly, she hears a voice singing along to her music.

Grandma looks around, but no one is there. So she goes to check if Kofi and Adjoa are still asleep.

Grandma quietly opens the door and finds Kofi and Adjoa fast asleep.

She smiles and goes back to the kitchen.

Grandma washes four plates, two cups, and a wooden spoon, singing happily. Then suddenly...

"Grandma I can't sleep and I just want to stay with you," Kofi said.

Grandma sighs and says, "But Kofi, I am tidying up and it's past your bedtime!"

Kofi frowns and goes back to the bedroom.

Kofi gets an idea. He sneaks into the bathroom to get the step that he uses to reach the sink when he brushes his teeth.

He puts the step in front of Grandma's huge wardrobe and carefully climbs onto it to reach the shelf where Grandma always keeps her special cloth.

OOOW!!!!

There were greens, reds, blues, yellows and even
shiny golds! The wardrobe is full of Grandma's
special cloths.

Kofi just could not choose, until he noticed,
a beautiful cloth right in front of him.
"I want this one!" he shouted as he pulled it out.

Kofi runs downstairs and into the kitchen.

Grandma jumped and said angrily, "Kofi, why are you not sleeping?"

"Grandma I have an idea! If you put me on your back, and tie me with this cloth, I can still be with you whilst you clean!" Kofi shouted.

Pleaaaaase!

Grandma is surprised! She looks at Kofi with a very serious face and then she smiles saying, "Of course you can!"

Grandma stretches out the cloth and picks Kofi up. She balances him carefully on her back and wraps the cloth around him.

"Grandma, how did you learn how to carry children on your back?" Kofi asks.

"I learned when I used to live in Ghana, but people all over the world carry their children on their backs too," Grandma replies. "Your great-grandmother used to carry me on her back when she used to go to the market."

"Grandma, what is this drawing?" Kofi asks.

Grandma says "This is an Adinkra symbol called 'Gye Nyame' it means EXCEPT FOR GOD. There are lots of Adinkra symbols and they all have different meanings."

"Wow...and Grandma..."

"No more questions Kofi, it is bedtime! We can look up the rest of the symbols tomorrow," says Grandma.

Kofi rests his head on Grandma's back and she continues to wash the plates whilst singing...

"Goodnight baby,
goodnight baby,
goodnight baby,
goodnight, goodnight,
goodnight."

And Kofi falls asleep.

Printed in Great Britain
by Amazon